## Newcastle Libraries and Information Service

☎ **0845 002 0336**

| Due for return | Due for return | Due for return |
| --- | --- | --- |
| 2 0 AUG 2012 | 2 0 JUN 2013 | |
| 2 8 AUG 2012 | | |
| 2 0 SEP 2012 | | |
| – 1 NOV 2012 | | |
| 2 8 FEB 2013 | | |
| 1 6 MAR 2013 | | |

Please return this item to any of Newcastle's Libraries by the last
date shown above. If not requested by another customer the loan
can be renewed, you can do this by phone, post or in person.
**Charges may be made for late returns.**

Other books by Nick Butterworth and Mick Inkpen

THE NATIVITY PLAY
THE SCHOOL TRIP
JUST LIKE JASPER
JASPER'S BEANSTALK

First published in 1988
by Hodder and Stoughton Children's Books

This edition published in 2007

Copyright © Nick Butterworth and Mick Inkpen 1988

Hodder Children's Books
338 Euston Road
London NW1 3BH

Hodder Children's Books Australia
Level 17/207 Kent Street
Sydney, NSW 2000

The rights of Nick Butterworth and Mick Inkpen to be identified as
the authors and illustrators of this Work have been asserted by them
in accordance with the Copyright, Designs and Patents Act 1988.

A catalogue record of this book is available from the British Library.

ISBN: 9780340932407
10 9 8 7 6 5 4 3 2

Printed in China

Hodder Children's Books is a division of Hachette Children's Books.
An Hachette Livre UK Company.

# THE
# SPORTS DAY

## NICK BUTTERWORTH
## AND
## MICK INKPEN

Hodder
Children's
Books

A division of Hachette Children's Books

Hooray! Today is Sports Day.
Sam is training hard. He's eaten all his breakfast
and now he's doing his exercises.
Tracy is still in bed. She says she's saving her
energy for later.

'Good luck,' says Dad as he goes off to work.
Mum is listening for the weather forecast.
'...and later on, showers spreading to all parts.'

It's a lovely afternoon. It looks like the
weatherman was wrong.
Lots of mums and dads have come to watch.
'Welcome to our Sports Day everybody,' says
Mrs Jefferson. But the loud hailer isn't working
properly and nobody can hear.
She gives it a shake and tries again. Still it
won't work.
Mr Bryant, the caretaker, comes to help.
He switches it on.

The first race is for the infants. It's a bean
bag race.
'Stand back behind the line,' says Miss Foster.
'Ready. Steady. Go!'
They're off.
Jeffrey's bean bag has fallen off his head.
Jenny's is slipping off too.
Matthew's won't come off. He's holding it on.

The next race is the wheelbarrow race.
'Now pushers, don't push too hard,' says Miss Foster.
'We don't want any broken wheels.'
David and Jamie are making a lot of noise.
'We're being a space buggy, Miss,'
says Jamie.
'Spacemen need to be extra careful,'
says Miss Foster.
Away they go!
Everybody shouts and cheers.
It's going to be close . . .
At the finish the space buggy
is just beaten by a
wheelbarrow.

Karen has to use special walking sticks to help her get about. She's going to run in the fifty metres dash. Miss Foster says that Karen can start a little in front if she likes. But Karen doesn't want to.
They're off and running.
Look at Karen go! She's going to come third.
Go on Karen!
There's a great big cheer as she crosses the line.
After the race everyone wants a go with Karen's walking sticks.

Sam and his friend Richard are revving up at the
starting line like two racing cars. Brrrmmm!
They're in the egg and spoon race.
Miss Foster says, 'Go!' and they're off.
The girls are going very carefully. Especially Tania.
She isn't going to be first. But she isn't going to
drop her egg.

Sam is doing well. Very well. He's going to win!
'Oh no!' Richard has dropped his egg and it's broken!
It's run all over his shoe.
One of the teachers wipes it off.
'Your mum was supposed to
give you a hard-boiled
egg,' she says.

Oh dear. Where have those clouds come from?
It looks like the weatherman was right after all.
Let's hope it's just a passing shower.
On go the coats. Up go the umbrellas.
Tracy's mum didn't bring an umbrella.
But she did bring a flask.
'Would you like some Miss Foster?'
'Thank you,' says Miss Foster. 'It's brightening up
a bit now.'

Good. The rain has stopped. The sun comes out and
the umbrellas start to steam.

Tracy is in the next race. It's the obstacle race.

'Run backwards to the hoops,' says Miss Foster, 'then
through the hoops, under the sheet, into the sacks
and hop to the finish.'

'Are you ready? Go!'

Tracy's off to a good start.
Oh dear. Joanne's got the hoop stuck.
Tracy's the first one under the sheet.
Matthew's found a hole in it.
Now what's happening?
There's a lot of wriggling and giggling under the sheet.
But no one's coming out.
'I think we'd better help them out,' says Miss Foster.
No one wins. But it was good fun.

The last race of the afternoon is the dads' race.
'My dad's a brilliant runner,' says Henry.
'So is mine,' says Paul.
The dads are all laughing as they wait for the start.
'Go!'
They're off. Oops! Henry's dad has lost a sandal.
Nicola's dad wins. Henry's dad is last.
'Don't cry Henry,' says Miss Foster.
But Henry says he's just got
something in his eye.

And now it's time to go home.
'Well done everybody,' says Mrs Jefferson, and she thanks everyone for coming. But no one can hear. Mr Bryant has put the loud hailer away.

'Did you see me win, Mum?' says Sam.
'I certainly did,' says Mum.
'Look, there's Dad!' shouts Tracy. 'Come on Sam. I'll race you to the gate!'